HOLIDAY COLLECTION

The Angel, the Spider, and the Christmas Tree

Alice Dare

Illustrations by Debora Weber

© 1996 Alice Dare

Illustrations by Debora Weber
Book design by Debora Weber and Claire Calhoun
Edited by Martha Pillow

First edition

Published by Bridge Resources
Louisville, Kentucky

PRINTED IN MEXICO

96 97 98 99 00 01 02 03 04 05 — 10 9 8 7 6 5 4 3 2 1

Long ago in the far northern woods, there lived a poor woman and her six children. The children's names were Molly, Holly, Polly, Peter, Deter, and Rollie. The woman's name was Mother. Well, really her name was Olga Gudstav, but the children called her Mother.

The family lived in a cabin that the children's father had built before he became ill with a bad fever and died. But even though it was rather bare inside, it was snug and warm on cold winter nights.

As those nights stretched longer and colder, the family began to think of Christmas.

"How will we celebrate?" asked Rollie, who was the youngest one.

"Of course we will go to church," said Holly.

"Of course we will have a tree," said Peter.

"Of course I will bake the Christmas cake," said Mother.

"Of course we will have presents," said Polly.

"How will we have presents," asked Deter, "when we don't have money to buy them and we don't even have enough time to make presents for everyone?"

"We can draw names," said Molly. "Then we can each make one present so we will give one and get one."

"Good idea," said Mother. She wrote each name on a scrap of paper and put the names in the pocket of her apron.

The children drew names and began thinking of what they would make and how they could keep all the gifts a secret.

Every night Molly, Holly, Polly, Peter, Deter, Rollie, and Mother worked on their gifts.

High up in a corner of the cabin, the warm corner behind the stovepipe, there lived a spider. To pay for her rent, she caught flies that came inside the cabin and ate them so they wouldn't buzz the children and their mother. From her home near the ceiling, the spider looked down every night and watched the family at work.

My, my, thought the spider. These people are busier than bees. They work harder than ants. I wonder what this Christmas is that they are getting ready for? (Spiders don't live as long as people, and this spider had never seen a Christmas.)

The day before Christmas the family was excited. "The Christmas tree! The Christmas tree!" chanted Rollie. "We're going to get the Christmas tree!"

The children left the cabin to tramp through the snowy forest, looking for just the right tree. Molly pulled the sled and Peter carried the ax. But Mother stayed home to bake the Christmas cake and some surprise Christmas cookies.

When the children returned, they had a beautiful tree. Mother helped them set it up, then they decorated it with what they had—turnips, parsnips, radishes, and apples.

"So that's a Christmas tree," said the spider from her high-up watching place.

Then the children and their mother brought the gifts they had made and wrapped, and put them under the tree. "Tell us about the Christmas Angel," said Rollie.

"Tonight," said Mother, "the Christmas Angel will come and look at the presents under the tree. If she sees that they are made with love, she will bless the gifts so they will always bring happiness to the people who receive them."

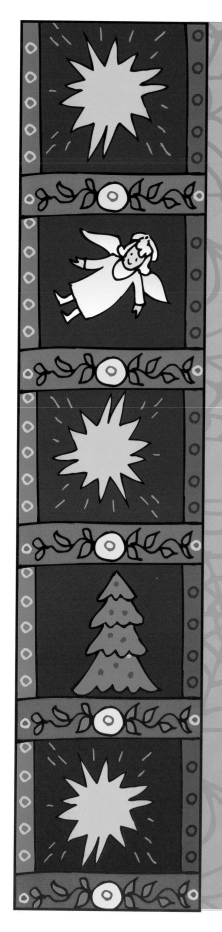

Late that night the family went to town to attend the midnight service of worship. The spider was so impressed with the family and their gifts that she decided she would surprise them with a present of her own. She crawled down the wall, across the floor, and had just crept up into the tree when there was a sudden bright light. She threw a leg up to shade her eyes and saw standing there in the middle of the room something—someone— like a person. Was it . . .? Yes, it must be. The Christmas Angel.

The Christmas Angel examined the tree. "Oh!" exclaimed the Angel. "A spider!"

How embarrassing! thought the spider.

"Spider! What are you doing in the Christmas tree?" asked the Angel.

The spider blushed. "I wanted to leave a little gift for the family."

"All right," said the Angel, a little annoyed. "But hurry up. I have to inspect the presents and then go to the next place. And when I leave, you cannot be in the tree. Whoever heard of a spider in a Christmas tree?"

The spider crawled as fast as she could to the top of the tree and then gracefully made her way around and down.

The Angel examined the gifts and saw how much love the family had put into the making of each one. She blessed the gifts and was ready to go.

"Spider?" called the Angel. "Are you out of the tree?"

"Yes," replied the spider, hurrying up the wall.

The Angel turned and looked up at the tree. "Oh no!" cried the Angel. "Spider! Look what you did. You ruined the tree! Why would you do a mean trick like that?"

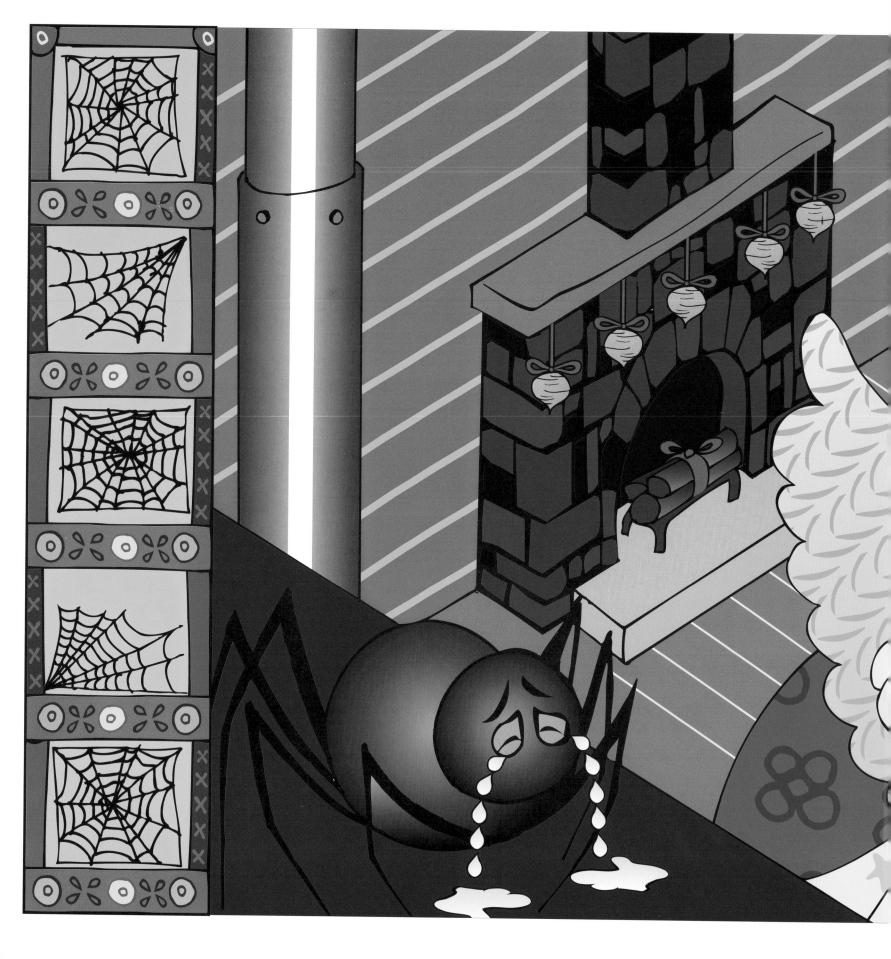

The spider was startled. A mean trick? Ruined the tree? The spider began to cry. "I didn't mean to," she moaned. "I made the most beautiful web I could. The only thing I can make is a web," said the spider. "It's the only gift I can give."

The Angel was humbled and she apologized. She looked again at the web draped all around the tree. "If I had taken the time . . ." said the Angel.

"I would have seen all the love you put into your gift. It is lovely. I am going to bless your gift just as I did the others."

When the family arrived home from church, Mother turned up the lamp and the spider's web shimmered and shone. "Look at our tree!" said Polly.

"It's the most beautiful tree in the world!" said Rollie.

And that is why, to this day, people decorate their Christmas trees with shiny silver strands.

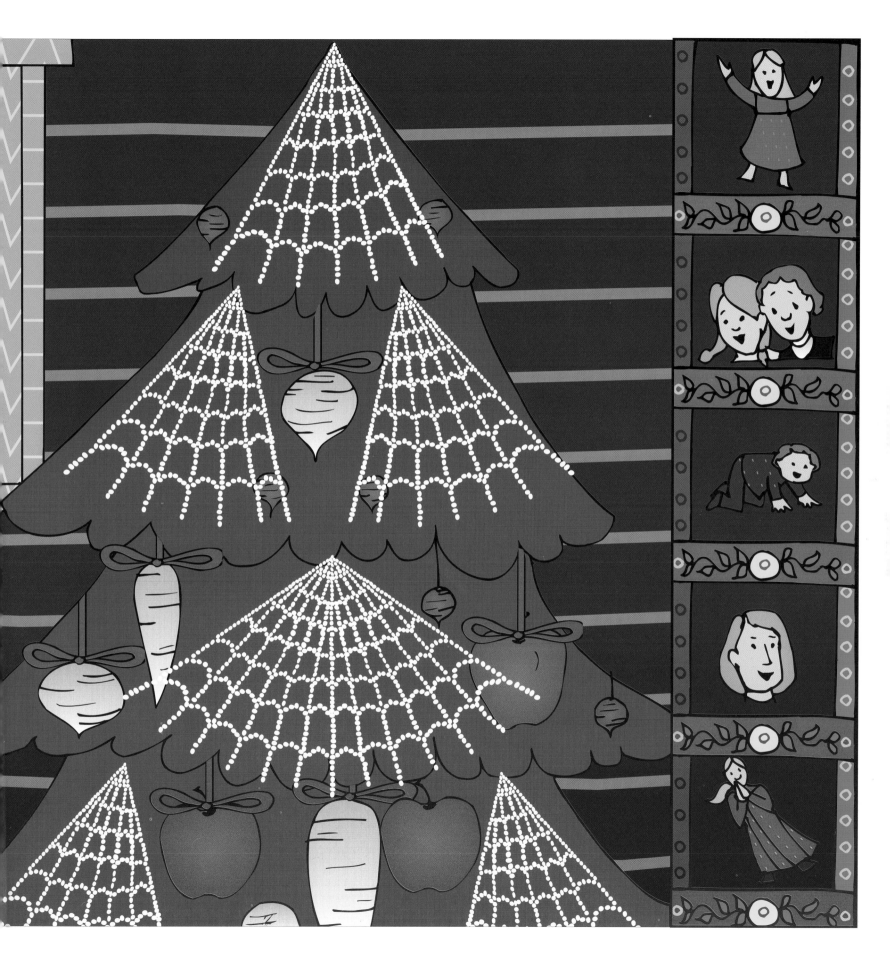

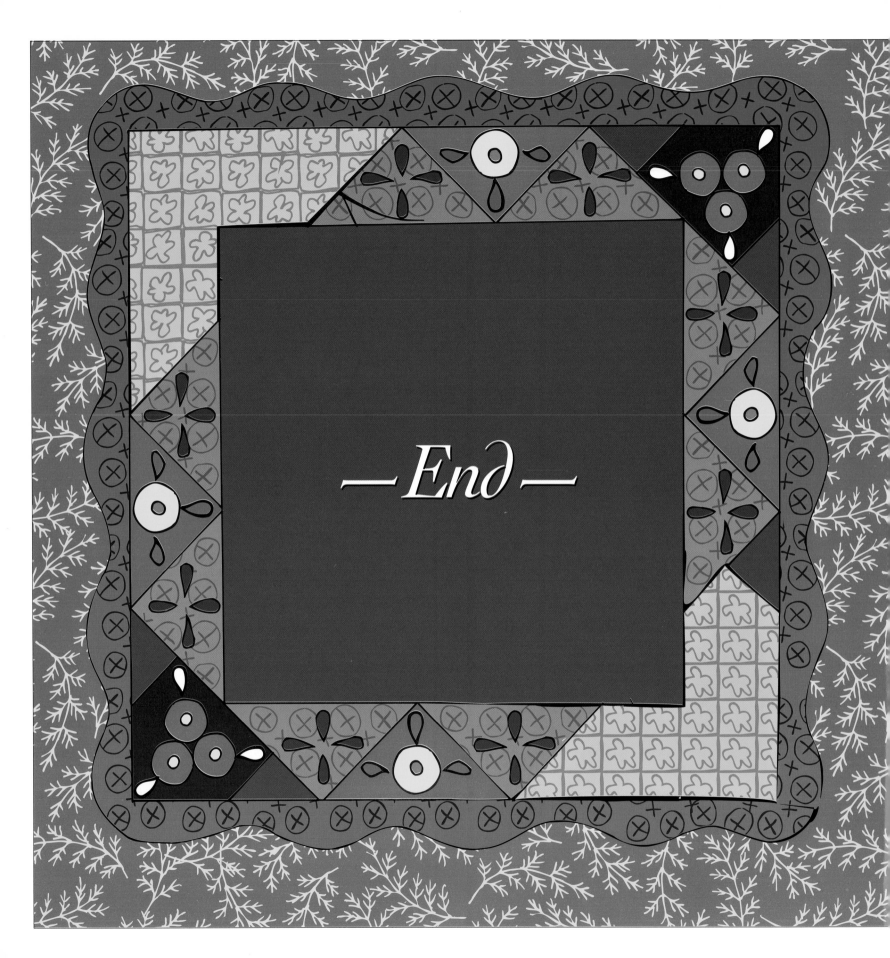

–End–